To my mischievous siblings,
who inspire me and fuel my
wicked sense of humour.

—B. W.

Published by
Peachtree Publishers
1700 Chattahoochee Avenue
Atlanta, Georgia 30318-2112
www.peachtree-online.com

First published in Great Britain in 2017 by Two Hoots, an imprint of Pan Macmillan
First United States version published in 2017 by Peachtree Publishers

Illustrations rendered in gouache on cartridge paper

Printed in April 2017 in China
10 9 8 7 6 5 4 3 2 1
First Edition

ISBN 978-1-68263-003-7

Cataloging-in-Publication Data is available from the Library of Congress.

Bethan Woollvin

Rapunzel

PEACHTREE
ATLANTA

Rapunzel lived all alone in a tall, dark tower.

She was trapped there by a witch, who visited every day.

"Rapunzel, Rapunzel, let down your hair!" the witch would call.

And then up Rapunzel's hair she climbed,

because that was the only way into the tower.

Every day, the witch brushed
Rapunzel's hair, *swish, swish.*

Then

Snip,
Snip,

she stole some golden locks to sell for riches.

As she left with her treasure, the witch always cackled, "You can never escape, Rapunzel! Leave the tower, and I will put a terrible curse on you!"

But was Rapunzel frightened? Oh no, not she!

If the witch could use her hair to get in,
Rapunzel could use it to get out.

So one day, she did.

After
climbing
down from
the tower,
Rapunzel pulled
her hair free
and looked around.
Then she started
to explore.

The idea of returning
to the tower made her sad.
It's a shame about that witch,
she thought.

So Rapunzel made a plan.
She worked on it secretly
every day.

And with the help of a
new friend from the forest,
she was always safely back
in the tower before the
witch came.

The witch never suspected a thing.

Until one day…

She saw the leaf in Rapunzel's hair.

"RAPUNZEL!"

But was Rapunzel frightened? Oh no, not she!
"The wind must have blown that in
through the window," she said.

"Well remember," snarled the witch,
"If I ever catch you leaving the
tower, I will put a TERRIBLE
curse on you."

And with that, she took hold of the end of Rapunzel's hair
and climbed out the window.

But the witch
didn't get far.

Snip

Snip

Rapunzel climbed out of the tower for the last time, and she never worried about a witch's curse again.

But were the witches frightened?

Oh yes, indeed!